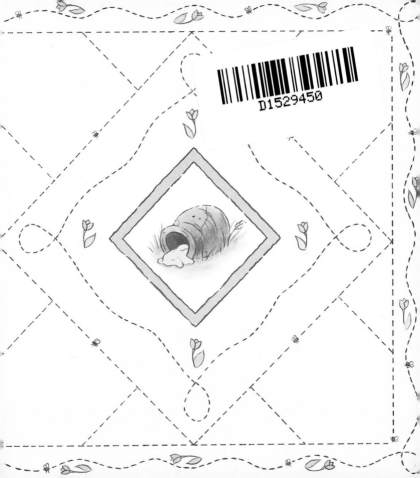

D1529450

So please accept this from . . . guess who!
A grateful friend and Winnie the Pooh!

The reason? Just because you're you!

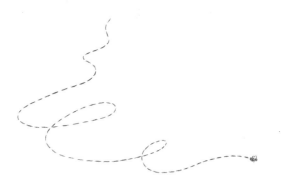

And every day, I thank you, too . . .

For spring flowers.

I thank the showers . . .

For April showers.

I thank the clouds . . .

I thank the trees.

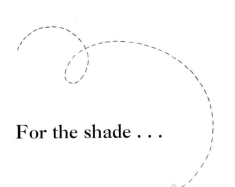

For the shade . . .

I thank the bees.

For the honey . . .

Winnie the Pooh thanks his friends Don Ferguson, J.J. Smith-Moore, Sparky Moore, and Diana Wakeman for helping to make this book.

THANK YOU

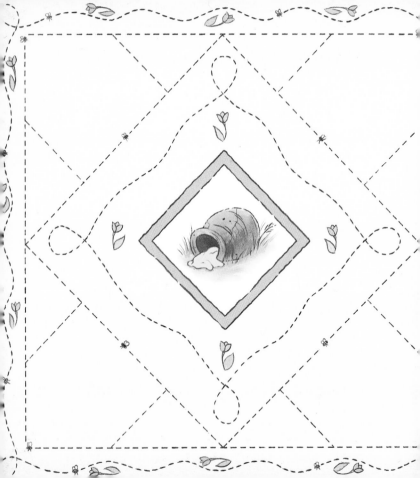